A Wedding Of Sorts

LIANA BROOKS

OTHER WORKS

ALL I WANT FOR CHRISTMAS

All I Want For Christmas Is A Reaper
All I Want For Christmas Is A Werewolf

FLEET OF MALIK

Bodies In Motion
Change of Momentum

HEROES AND VILLAINS

Even Villains Fall In Love
Even Villains Go To The Movies
Even Villains Have Interns
Even Villains Play The Hero (books 1 – 3 omnibus)
The Polar Terror

TIME AND SHADOWS

The Day Before
Convergence Point
Decoherence

SHORTER WORKS

Fey Lights
Prime Sensations
Darkness and Good

Find other works by the author at
www.lianabrooks.com

A Wedding Of Sorts

INKLET #74

LIANA BROOKS

Inkprint PRESS

www.inkprintpress.com

Print ISBN: 978-1-922434-14-2
eBook ISBN: 9798201274924

www.inkprintpress.com

National Library of Australia Cataloguing-in-Publication Data
Brooks, Liana 1982 –
A Wedding Of Sorts
34 p.
ISBN: 978-1-922434-14-2
Inkprint Press, Canberra, Australia
1. Fiction—Fantasy—Contemporary 2. Fiction—Fairy Tales, Folk Tales, Legends & Mythology 3. Fiction—Short Stories

First Print Edition: January 2022
Cover photo © Selenittt via Deposit Photos
Cover design © Inkprint Press
Interior art © Amy Laurens

A WEDDING OF SORTS

In retrospect, telling a narcissist that I'd rather die than marry him was —perhaps—a touch theatrical. People like Prince Jarmien tend to take threats to their ego badly.

My dress of pale ivory with forget-me-knots embroidered on the hem attempted to flutter in the pre-dawn breeze. It managed a feeble flap, but the mud on the hem weighed it down. It was a damp sort of morning, lacking the dramatic red sunrise the cliffs were known for.

Sullen clouds clustered on the horizon, their whispering, conspiring breezes whipping the waves below into a frenzy.

White caps of foam lashed against the gray stone of the cliffs, beating a steady tattoo.

I turned, bare feet sinking another inch into the cold mud.

The prince should have waited a few more weeks. Winter's frost had barely retreated, leaving the fields soggy messes of bare, boggy earth and scraggly weeds.

In another month the hills would be a luscious, emerald green and dotted with fallen stars, poppies, and buttercups.

Fallen stars with their five, almost translucent, pearly white petals would have made a beautiful crown for a bride.

My crown was ivy, which seemed a little clingy and ill-considered to me.

And it didn't match the dress at all.

Not that anyone had asked.

After I'd declared I'd rather die than marry, I'd been locked in the uppermost tower for three weeks with little food and less company.

Now I stood at the edge of the cliffs, barefoot and wearing a too-large dress with an itchy crown of poking ivy in front of an assembly of the prince's court. Most of them were sensibly dressed in heavy wool and fur coats, the colors running from deep reds for the nobles to rich browns with golden accents for the men-at-arms.

The prince was not a poor man.

No, and unlike the maidens standing to the side and letting tears drip past their veils, I was not wealthy.

I had magic.

Or so the prince believed.

Gold would feed his armies, but magic would win the war with his brother—at least according to the mystic who'd put this whole notion into his head.

I looked at him, a reedy man with thinning brown hair and a horse's long face. His eyes were small and dark, filled with anger and madness.

He stepped forward, lips stretching into a thin smile. "Now, do you see what your choices are? Wedded bliss or death. Choose: me or the cliffs."

I leaned forward to look at the angry waves below. "You realize this isn't at all necessary."

"Silence, witch!" The prince vibrated with pent up anger. "Your magic must me mine before the first eve of spring."

Ah, that explained the wedding in the mud then.

Putting on a placating smile, I turned. "Prince, noble and beloved of..." I looked at the grumpy assembly "...beloved of the people. I am not a witch. I have told you and your men and your women and everyone, in fact, that I have no magic. If I did, I would not have sat in a cold tower for weeks!"

"You have magic," the prince insisted, his small eyes narrowing into gimlets of fury. "You will marry me and give it to me."

"Please!" I rushed toward him and dropped to the cold mud. "Please, my prince, have mercy. I am but a humble farm girl. I have no magic. I have no gifts to save you with. I beg of you, allow me to go free and marry another. Marry for love."

Behind him one of the maidens sobbed loud enough to be heard over the crashing waves.

A gull screeched in the sky overhead, heralding the coming dawn.

"You are loved by another," I told the prince. "What magic could replace that? What power could a humble daughter of the dirt have?"

Rough fingers grabbed my arm and dragged me to my feet.

"You will marry me," the prince said. "The blood of our wedding bed will give the magic I need to conquer."

"Blood?" My free hand reached and my fingers caught the hilt of his dagger. "Is it my blood you want, prince?"

Pushing away, I stripped the dagger from him and ran it across my arm, laying bear the bright red life blood of my veins. "Take it." I shoved my arm forward. "Take the blood you desire, but leave me my name! I beg of you. Kill me but leave me a maiden."

He reached for me and my numb feet slipped on the mud.

I'd leaned too far, and too late I realized I wasn't simply falling away from him, but falling down.

The cold spray of the ocean rushed passed me, pulled me under with a lover's touch, drowning me far from the sunbeams breaking over the clouds on the horizon.

Violent currents spun me around, crushed the air out of me, ripped the dress from my limbs.

I kicked free of the hated gown. Swam down and let the saltwater fill my lungs. Swam further until the human skin sloughed from my limbs and left the radiance of scales, pale and glimmering like fallen star flowers.

Hours later, I settled on the rocky ground beneath the waves, near the wrecks of ships that had dared to trespass in my family's territory.

All right.

So I'd lied to the prince.

I did have magic.

Not the kind he needed to win the war with his brother, but magic enough to give me a woman's face as I hunted for a husband. My kind birthed no sons. It wasn't the nature of the sea to make men. If I wanted children to sing more ships into the deep with me, I'd have to find my own man, make him fall in love, and change him so he was more like me.

A bubble escaped my lips with a sigh.

Well, clearly the prince wasn't the man for me, and I couldn't go back to his kingdom any time soon.

That was all right. There would be other centuries to pluck men from. And then?

I ran a hand across the sharp barnacles clinging to the wrecks of the sunken ships.

Then I would sing a song and grow my garden of death beneath the waves.

THE MAKING OF
A WEDDING OF
SORTS

I wrote this short story because I'd been toying with the idea of a contemporary fantasy series with a siren and I couldn't quite make it work. I love the idea of the beautiful woman singing doomed sailors to her. It's a haunting thought. One that perhaps brought comfort to the families waiting at home for a ship to come in.

It wasn't the sailor's fault he left. Surely he didn't abandon me. He was tricked, by the evil siren luring men away, otherwise he'd come home to me today.

Re-watching the old *Three Musketeers* with Lady de Winter solidified the idea of the story in my head. Why would a woman throw herself from a cliff for any reason unless she thought she could survive?

Perhaps she did. Perhaps the lady swam home.

Read more by Liana Brooks!

ALL I WANT FOR CHRISTMAS IS A REAPER

THREE O'CLOCK ON A THURSDAY AFTERNOON IN APRIL, and I had an unplanned three-day weekend. In Chicago, my favorite city in the world. There were thunderheads gathering over Lake Michigan with the smell of rain in the air but, for now, downtown was a delightful playground of rushing cars, stressed commuters, and the bitter tears of lives I'd ruined with a pink slip.[1]

With nowhere in particular to be, I meandered, crossing Clark Street at the light to reach a small city park with maple trees that

---

[1] Technically this is a lie. Dulcie Waterhouse ruined her own life by embezzling from her firm and taking too many long lunch breaks buying macarons across town. The only tears were the tears of joy in her co-workers' eyes when they realized she was leaving for good. And there wasn't a pink slip. I convinced her to resign. I'm good like that.

wouldn't reach maturity in this century, a little playground with a sun shade, and a recycled rubber tire running track that crossed through the limited greenspace like a drunken snake trying to bite its own tail.

It was too early for school to be out and too late for lunch, which meant the park was populated by a muddy handful of toddlers, their attendant adults, and me. I kept to the outside track, crossing a stone footbridge over a shallow dirt ditch that might become a small pond if it rained. Tulips bobbed in the wind. The forsythia was out.

Little flowers and cheeky sparrows.

I enjoyed it for about four minutes before I could feel my brain scrabbling around like a trapped rat desperate for escape.

Natural vistas had that effect on me. I needed something to think about. A job to focus on. Numbers. Problems. City things.

At the sound of a jogger approaching, I stepped to the side so they could sweep past and catch the running track.

And sweep past he did. A gloriously muscular runner with olive-toned tan skin, a shock of silver-white hair shaved on the sides and long on top, a well-defined back and legs, and a black shirt sliding out of his waistband and dropping to the ground.

Well then.

It wasn't quite the young Miss Bennet dropping her gloves so a militia man could retrieve them for her, but it was possibly the twenty-first century equivalent. Even if it wasn't, it was only polite to collect the handsome man's shirt and return it to him.

I picked it up, shook off the dust and grass clippings, and held the sandalwood-scented shirt up for inspection. The owner was broad shouldered and the shirt was lean cut, meant to hug him and give everyone looking an excellent view of his well-defined muscles. Slightly more interesting was the word KILLER written across the front of the shirt in the font of the well-known horror brand, Slasher.

The jogger was a scary movie fan.

Not a lot to work with as openings went.

Scary movies weren't my cup of cocoa. No movies were, most days. Sitting still for hours on end listening to other people talk made me restless.

Perhaps it wasn't meant to be.

I folded the shirt neatly, and when I

looked up the jogger was watching me from the bend of the running track only a few feet away, one white earbud hanging off his shoulder, the other still in his ear. He was younger than the white hair suggested, maybe twenties or early thirties, with dark brown—nearly black—eyes, high cheek-bones, a well-defined jaw line, and a sharp, straight nose. He looked exceptionally intense and unquantifiably captivating.

"Is that my shirt?" he asked in a deep voice as delicious as he was. I could listen to that man read the dictionary and I'd love every moment of it.

I held the shirt up, letting it unfurl over my dress. "I don't know, do you think it's mine?" I let him get a good look at me. Large, dark reds curls that looked a century out of date, a pink flower tucked behind my ear, pink lipstick, pretty smile, A-line green dress with pink flowers embroidered on it and a crinoline underneath for volume; I looked like a piece of walking history.

Twee. Sweet. Friendly.

Stupid.

I'd heard every verdict, but the dress made me look fabulous and I loved bringing a pop of cheer to people's otherwise blighted lives.

"It'd look good on you. Killer." The corner of his mouth lifted in a sexy smile.

Oh. *No*. I did *not* like that.

Actually, I did, very much, but I knew where sexy smiles led. It would be hot nightclubs, wild parties, and then a trip to the suburbs as Mr. Sexy waxed lyrical about 'getting away from the city.' Pretty soon he'd be browsing baby name websites and talking about getting a dog.

No.

If a *Timberwolf Town*[2] werewolf couldn't tempt me, then a yappy little dog suitable for the suburbs didn't stand a chance.

I held the shirt to my shoulders and tried not to notice how good it smelled—sandalwood with an undertone of mint. The scent was too light for a cologne—probably a soap. "It looks like my size, too." Assuming it was

---

[2] A paranormal-horror series from the mid 20s that centered around a hidden werewolf population and their unrivaled basketball team. I'm 90% certain that the ratings were due to the regular shower scenes.

supposed to be worn halfway to my knees. Jogging, dark, and handsome was also tall, dark, and handsome.

"I'll let you borrow it some time." The man had dark, hungry eyes that promised to make my flirtation worth my time.

"Sure." That was never going to happen. I tossed the shirt to him. "Enjoy your run."

The smile turned to a smirk. "Enjoy the view." He secured the shirt to his waistband again and took off with a wink.

Confidence was always sexy, and I was very tempted to continue my little stroll around the park and see if the jogger wanted to join me for a post-workout snack somewhere.

I was great at first dates. Lots of confidence and a big smile got me everything I wanted.

Second dates?

No one had tempted me enough to schedule a second date since college.

I glanced at the jogger again. *Maybe* no one had tempted me?

He looked familiar in that we–met–once–in–passing sort of way.

My memory for names and faces was legendary, but I couldn't recall being introduced to him before.

It was going to bother me all afternoon if I didn't pursue it.

As if the office had a psychic link,[3] my phone rang, the quick staccato tattoo reserved for my boss. Work was there again, to rescue me from my worst impulses and save me from the kind of heartbreak ice cream couldn't fix.

"Hi, Amara." I moved toward the crosswalk, dodging a little green car that nearly swerved into me.

Chicago drivers. So charming.

There was a tiny community garden space across the street, a safe distance from the sexy jogger.

"Merri, I just heard the good word from Windy City Security, you've officially slayed the wicked witch of the upper west side. Did you break seven minutes?" Amara Rosa

---

[3] Or, let's be honest, a stopwatch to keep track of the betting on the Dulcie Waterhouse situation.

Park[4] was just as competitive as I was and she'd had my back in the office betting pool.

Sloan and Markham is *the* name in corporate accounting in Illinois. Amara is the head of the forensic accounting unit.

Really, we're a bunch of math nerds who read too many mystery novels and decided we'd grow up to fight white collar crime for a six-figure annual salary. And in the land of the nerds, I'm the big, brutal boss, the final, unconquerable hurdle.

"Six minutes," I said with a killer smile.[5]

"You make me so happy! Did Dulcie cry? I met her when I went in for the initial contact and…" Amara sighed. "Some people just *look* evil, you know?"

I pictured Dulcie Waterhouse in her gray pantsuit with a black silk shell under the jacket, two silver studs in each ear, a professional, asymmetrical cut for her dark brown hair, and dark red lipstick on a mouth pouring out more cuss words than could fit into

---

[4] Named for Amara Enyia and Rosa Parks, obviously.

[5] Ha ha, I'm so funny!

a Monday morning commute when the trains were down. "She didn't cry, but you may need to give the interns a bonus for reading my emails for the next few weeks."

"More death threats?" Amara sighed again. "What is it about you that attracts so much venom?"

"It's the job." And the fact that dressing like the lead singer from a retro throwback band made everyone underestimate me. What can I say? I have brains *and* beauty.

With a click of her tongue, Amara dismissed the disappointing news. "Well, done is done. I'll give the interns a heads up." There was a chime in the background. "Oh, and there's the first hit on social media. Want to hear it?"

"It's not like I'm going to look it up." I didn't do social media. Despite having an email assigned to me along with my social security number, I had the digital footprint of a ghost.

"The headline is 'Chicago's Infamous Grim Reaper Strikes Again.' Good job."

"I try my best."

Amara made a happy, purring sound. "Did you try your very best with Harry?"

"Harry?" I stopped in front of a bench. "I'm drawing a blank."

"Junior executive in accounting?" Amara dangled the tidbit.

Mentally I flipped through a detailed list of junior accounting people. "Not ringing any bells."

"Henderson account?"

I shuddered.

"He sent you a gorgeous bouquet of day lilies—"

"He was telling me about how his parents were building a new house in Sugar Grove and how the commute was under thirty minutes to the city with the new high-speed trains."

There was a stunned silence and then Amara took a deep breath. "So…"

"So, thanks but no thanks? Give them to someone else."

"He left a note too."

Stupid man. But it was only polite to read the note and find some excuse for why I couldn't show up to Domestication Of The Wild Wifey 101. "Leave it on my desk. I'll deal with it when I get back to the office."

"About that…."

"You have another job for me before the weekend?" If there were gods who smiled fondly on math nerds, I would have prayed. Numbers and patterns were my favorite candy. A weekend sorting through someone else's finances as just as blissful as a bubble bath.

There was a hesitant little sigh, which meant Amara wasn't sold on the job but someone was begging. "This is an odd one. It's not the bosses calling, it's an employee, and she asked for you by name because she said you worked here, but she didn't seem to know what it is you do."

Weird. "The name?"

"Ellen Berry."

Someone else would have a hazy memory of a schoolyard friend who they'd met during a game of tag–turned–head–on–collision in kindergarten.

My memory was sharper than that, and off the top of my head I could rattle off all the major life events in Ellen's personal history up until she left for college in New York. We hadn't kept in touch mostly because I forgot people existed when I was working with math.

It was great for my bank account, but not for relationships.

"Merri?" Amara waited. "If I give you the address can you go over and see what's going on?"

"Sure. Where am I headed?"

"Cozy Studios—"

"Cozy as in Cozy TV with the candy-dipped romances?" Good grief. "Can I fire the writers for their poor plotlines?"

"Only if they're embezzling," Amara said. "Otherwise, give them the quick two-day special. A little workflow advice. A little hiring advice. And then get out of there, because we have the Oretega account to tackle next week."

Easy as mud pie in Mississippi. "Got it. In. Out. Tear-free."

"If you make it tear-free, I will personally buy you dinner anywhere in the city."

"I like expensive food," I warned.

"Cozy was just bought out by Slasher Corp," Amara reported with maybe just a soupçon of glee. "You're getting called in because Cozy is getting killed."

Keep reading! Head to
<u>www.inkprintpress.com/
lianabrooks/christmas/reaper/</u>
to buy your copy now!

ABOUT THE AUTHOR

LIANA BROOKS has never been given the choice between marriage and death, but nevertheless she does enjoy diving into the ocean at any opportunity. She also enjoys writing science fiction in every form, from sprawling space operas (*Fleet of Malik*) and time travel murder mysteries (*Time & Shadows*) to the antics of a superhero family (*Heroes and Villains*), as well as paranormal romances (*All I Want For Christmas*) and more.

You can find Liana online at www.lianabrooks.com, and on Twitter as @LianaBrooks.

INKLETS

Collect them all! Released on the 1st and 15th of each month.

INKLET #013
Shadows
NEVER LIE
AMY LAURENS

INKLET #080
Here She Lies
LIANA BROOKS

INKLET #081
Perfect
Destruction
An Age Of Unicorns Story
AMY LAURENS

INKLET #082
What Blood
Can Do
AMY LAURENS

INKLET #083
Dancer, Dreamer
Seer
LIANA BROOKS

INKLET #084
As Time
Whirls Slowly
Past
AMY LAURENS

INKLET #085
Far More
Satisfying
Than Hell
AMY LAURENS

INKLET #086
Just
Another Day
In Hell
LIANA BROOKS

INKLET #087
Moon AND
Morning
AMY LAURENS

INKLET #094
ANUBIS
Has Sent You
Six Souls
LIANA BROOKS

INKLET #095
PRAYER TO A
GODDESS
LIANA BROOKS

9 781922 434142